CROSS-COUNTRY SKIING

SKIING

THE STORY OF CANADIANS  IN THE OLYMPIC WINTER GAMES

Written by Blaine Wiseman

Weigl

Published by Weigl Educational Publishers Limited
6325 10 Street SE
Calgary, Alberta
T2H 2Z9

www.weigl.com

Library and Archives Canada Cataloguing in Publication data available upon request.
Fax 403-233-7769 for the attention of the Publishing Records department.

ISBN 978-1-55388-945-8 (hard cover)
ISBN 978-1-55388-954-0 (soft cover)

Printed in the United States of America
1 2 3 4 5 6 7 8 9 0   13 12 11 10 09

Editor: Heather C. Hudak
Design: Terry Paulhus

All of the Internet URLs given in the book were valid at the time of publication. However, due to the dynamic nature of the Internet,
some addresses may have changed, or sites may have ceased to exist since publication. While the author and publisher regret any
inconvenience this may cause readers, no responsibility for any such changes can be accepted by either the author or the publisher.

Every reasonable effort has been made to trace ownership and to obtain permission to reprint copyright material. The publishers would
be pleased to have any errors or omissions brought to their attention so that they may be corrected in subsequent printings.

Weigl acknowledges Getty Images as its primary image supplier for this title.

We gratefully acknowledge the financial support of the Government of Canada through the Book Publishing Industry Development
Program (BPIDP) for our publishing activities.

Contents

What are the Olympic Winter Games?

The Olympic Games began more than 2,000 years ago in the town of Olympia in Ancient Greece. The Olympics were held every four years in August or September and were a showcase of **amateur** athletic talent. The games continued until 393 AD, when they were stopped by the Roman emperor.

The Olympics were not held again for more than 1,500 years. In 1896, the first modern Olympics took place in Athens, Greece. The Games were the idea of Baron Pierre de Coubertin of France. Though these Games did not feature any winter sports, in later years, sports such as ice skating and ice hockey were played at the Olympics.

In 1924, the first Olympic Winter Games were held at Chamonix, France. The Games featured 16 nations, including Canada, the United States, Finland, France, and Norway. There were 258 athletes competing in 16 events, which included skiing, ice hockey, and speed skating. The first gold medal in a winter sport was awarded to speed skater Charles Jewtraw of the United States in the 500-metre event.

Cross-country skiing is showcased in 12 events at the Winter Olympic Games. One of these is the biathlon, which features a combination of cross-country skiing and target shooting. Cross-country skiing events can be long-distance trials, such the 50-kilometre race, shorter sprint races, or team relay events. Thorleif Haug of Norway won the first gold medal for cross-country skiing during the 1924 Winter Games.

TOP 10 MEDAL-WINNING COUNTRIES

COUNTRY	MEDALS
Norway	280
United States	216
USSR	194
Austria	185
Germany	158
Finland	151
Canada	119
Sweden	118
Switzerland	118
Democratic Republic of Germany	110

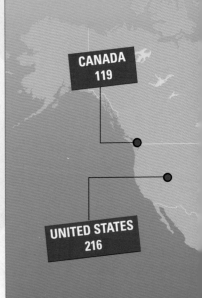

CANADA 119

UNITED STATES 216

Whistler Olympic Park
Parc olympique de Whistler

🍁 **CANADIAN TIDBIT** Vancouver will be the third Canadian city to host the Olympic Games. Montreal hosted the Summer Games in 1976, and Calgary hosted the Winter Games in 1988.

Winter Olympic Sports

Currently, there are seven Olympic winter sports, with a total of 15 **disciplines**. All 15 disciplines are listed here. In addition, there are five Paralympic Sports. These are alpine skiing, cross-country skiing, **biathlon**, ice sledge hockey, and wheelchair curling.

Alpine Skiing

Biathlon

Bobsleigh

Cross-Country Skiing

Curling

Figure Skating

Freestyle Skiing

Ice Hockey

Luge

Nordic Combined

Short Track Speed Skating

Skeleton

Ski Jumping

Snowboarding

Speed Skating

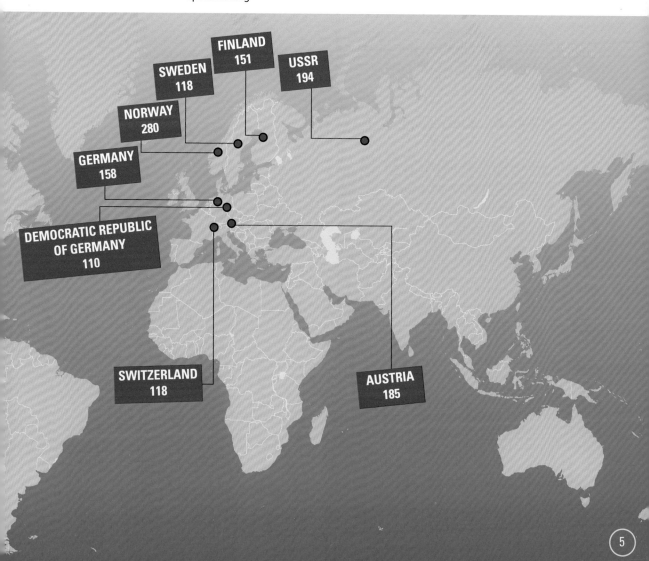

FINLAND 151

SWEDEN 118

USSR 194

NORWAY 280

GERMANY 158

DEMOCRATIC REPUBLIC OF GERMANY 110

SWITZERLAND 118

AUSTRIA 185

Canadian Olympic Cross-Country Skiing

The first people to cross-country ski were the Vikings of **Scandinavia** more than 4,000 yeas ago. Using skis, the Vikings could glide across the snow, making travel much easier. Cross-country skiing became a common way for people to hunt. Eventually, people began cross-country skiing for fun and in competition with others. Canada's first cross-country ski club was founded in 1891, in Revelstoke, British Columbia.

Beckie Scott took part in the Women's 5-kilometre Classical Cross-country during Winter Olympics in Salt Lake City, Utah.

The first Winter Olympics included cross-country skiing, but no Canadians participated. During the second Winter Olympics, in 1928, Canada was represented by two cross-country skiers. Out of 44 skiers, William Thompson finished in 37th place, while Merritt Putnam finished 40th. Although they did not win any medals, Thompson and Putnam had helped to put Canada on the winter sporting map. Canada has been represented in cross-country skiing at every Winter Olympics since.

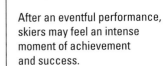

After an eventful performance, skiers may feel an intense moment of achievement and success.

The 1932 Winter Olympics in Lake Placid, New York, was a breakthrough for Canadian cross-country skiers. Kaare Engstad of Burns Lake, British Columbia, finished 19th in the 50-kilometre event. This remains Canada's best performance in that event. Camrose, Alberta's Jostein Nordmoe finished the **nordic combined** event in 10th place. This remained the pinnacle of Canada's cross-country skiing achievements for more than 50 years, until the Canadian women's relay team finished ninth in 1988.

Canada's greatest cross-country skiing moment to date came at the Winter Olympics in 2002, in Salt Lake City, Utah.

The medal is symbolic of the high sense of achievement felt by athletes such as Beckie Scott and Sara Renner.

The official poster for the 1928 Winter Olympic Games in St. Moritz, Switzerland, has been placed in the Olympic Museum n Lausanne, Switzerland.

Beckie Scott, of Vermillion, Alberta, became the first North American woman to win a cross-country skiing medal, taking gold in the **pursuit** event. She also finished in the top 10 spots in each of her other events.

In 2006, Scott and her teammate, Sara Renner, won the silver medal in the team sprint event. At that same Olympics, Canada won its second cross-country skiing gold medal. Competing in her first Olympics, Chandra Crawford, of Canmore, Alberta, finished in first place to win the gold medal in the 1.1-kilometre sprint in Turin, Italy.

🍁 **CANADIAN TIDBIT** During the 2002 Games, Beckie Scott was originally awarded the bronze medal in the ladies' 5-km combined pursuit. After competing in other events, the second and first place finishers were disqualified from the Games, and Scott was later awarded silver. More than two years later, Beckie Scott was awarded the gold medal at a ceremony in Vancouver. She is the only athlete in Olympic history to be awarded all three medals for the same race.

All the Right Equipment

Cross-country skiers glide across the snow on two skis, using poles to help push themselves along. Special equipment helps cross-country skiers use small amounts of energy to move across the snow as fast and as far as possible.

Skis are long, slim boards that are strapped to each foot. The skis balance the weight of the person wearing them, allowing skiers to stay on top of the snow instead of sinking. In the past, cross-country skis were simple planks of wood strapped to the skier's feet. Today, skis are made of lightweight materials, such as fibreglass, and have metal edges that dig into the snow when the skier takes a stride. Cross-country skis do not rest flat against the snow but flex slightly upward under the skier's foot. This is called camber, and it helps the skier push more powerfully and glide farther. Applying wax to the bottom of cross-country skis helps skiers glide across the snow more easily.

Skiers wear special boots that help their feet stay sturdy. The boot is attached to the ski with a device called a binding. Cross-country bindings only connect the boot to the ski near the toe. This allows athletes to lift their heel when they take a stride.

SKIS

Cross-country skiers wear special clothing that will help to protect their bodies, as well as enhance the quality of their performance.

Cross-country skiers must use the correct gear to help them glide across the snow or ice as fast as possible.

Before the 1850s, cross-country skiers only used one wooden pole to help push on both sides of their body. However, having two poles allows skiers to push themselves along more easily. Placing one pole into the snow and pushing with their arm, as well as the opposite leg, is the most efficient technique. Like today's skis, poles are made of lightweight, sturdy materials. This allows skiers to use the maximum amount of strength without breaking their equipment.

Since cross-country skiing is a winter sport that is performed outdoors, skiers must wear clothing that protects them from cold weather. Olympic cross-country skiers wear special, tight-fitting, **aerodynamic** suits that reduce air resistance and keep them warm.

CANADIAN TIDBIT At the Winter Olympics in 2006, in Turin, Italy, Canadian skier Sara Renner's poles broke in half during the team sprint event. Bjornar Hakensmoen, a Norwegian cross-country skiing coach who had never met the Canadian team, handed Renner a pole, helping her finish the race. Although the pole was far longer than Renner's pole had been, she was able to complete the race and win the silver medal for Canada. Hakensmoen's Norwegian team finished in fourth place.

Qualifying to Compete

George Grey and Alex Harvey of Canada finished third in the Men's 6 x 1.6K F Team Sprint at the 2009 FIS Cross Country World Cup.

Qualifying for the Canadian Olympic team takes a great deal of dedication and hard work. Skiers must perform at a high level in the years leading up to the Olympics if they want to be chosen for the national team. Skiers must complete several criteria before they can compete in the Olympics.

There are a certain number of available spots for skiers in each Olympic competition. These spots are divided among the competing nations, which then select the skiers who will represent them at the Olympics. Canada is allowed to send a total of 20 cross-country skiers to the Olympics. The team must be made up of men and women, with no more than 12 of either gender. In order to qualify, a skier must achieve at least 100 points in an International Ski Federation (FIS) event within two years of the Olympics. The higher skiers finish in an FIS race, the more points they are awarded for that race.

If a country does not have any skiers that have achieved this qualification standard, the skier it sends to the Olympics must have participated in at least five FIS competitions. However, in this case, the country can only send one skier to the Olympics.

On February 19, 2009, Sara Renner competed in the women's cross-country 10-kilometre Individual classic race at the FIS Nordic World Ski Championships in Czech Republic.

Skiers must meet or beat FIS qualifying times set for each event in order to make the nation's Olympic team.

OFFICIALS

At Olympic cross-country skiing competitions, there are several officials. Each official performs specific duties that help the competition run smoothly. A group of officials representing the FIS makes sure that the competition is prepared and executed properly. These officials are the technical delegate and an assistant, jury members, and a race director. The technical delegate is the highest official, making sure all aspects of the event are properly organized. The technical delegate appoints a chief of competition, who is in charge of how the event is conducted and judged. This official appoints other officials for the event and makes sure that they are qualified to do their jobs properly. Officials appointed by the chief of competition include the chief of course, who makes sure the course is in good condition, and chief of timekeeping. The jury decides if the weather is suitable to conduct the race and what happens to competitors if they break a rule. Jury members make decisions by voting on issues. The race director is in charge of all aspects of the race and ensures that the event is run according to FIS rules.

Rules of Cross-Country Skiing

There are 12 different cross-country skiing events featured at the Olympic Winter Games. These events are separated into men's and women's categories. The men's events include the 1.5-kilometre sprint, 10-kilometre pursuit, 15-kilometre and 30-kilometre mass starts, and the 50-kilometre and 4-by-10-kilometre relays. The women's events include the 1.5-kilometre sprint, 5-kilometre pursuit, 10-kilometre and 15-kilometre mass starts, and the 30-kilometre and 4-by-5-kilometre relays.

Sprint events are raced individually, with each skier starting the event 15 seconds after the previous skier. The fastest 16 athletes move to the quarter-final event. The top two skiers from each quarter-final move on to the semi-finals, and the top two from each semi-final race move to the finals. In the final event, the top three finishers win medals.

In mass start events, all competitors start at the same time. In these races, the first skier to cross the finish line is the winner.

The pursuit events feature a mass start. In these events, skiers use two skiing techniques, each requiring different equipment. The classical technique is a running-style of skiing in which the skis stay side-by-side. The free technique is more like skating, where the skier's strides push out to the side. Halfway through the race, the skiers stop to change their equipment.

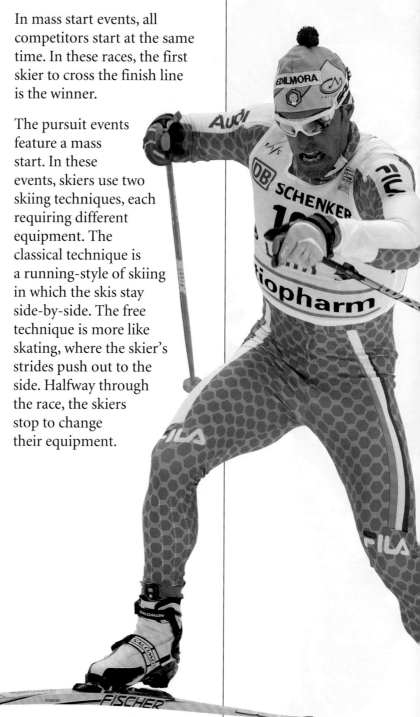

Skiers are not allowed to start a race before the official decides they can. They are also not permitted to interfere with other skiers. Officials understand that accidents can happen, but skiers must still compete fairly and responsibly.

Relay events feature teams of four skiers. Each skier skis one section, or leg, of the race. For example, in the 4-by-10-kilometre relay, four team members ski 10 kilometres each. The first team to complete 40 kilometres wins the race.

In Olympic cross-country skiing competitions, skiers must follow certain rules. Skiers must obey the officials before, during, and after all competitions. If a skier breaks any rule, the officials will punish that person accordingly. This may mean being penalized or disqualified from the competition.

PERFORMANCE ENHANCING DRUGS

Although the Olympics are a celebration of excellence and sportsmanship, some athletes use performance enhancing drugs to given them an unfair advantage over other athletes. There are many different types of performance enhancing drugs, including steroids. Some make muscles bigger, others help muscles recover more quickly, while some can make athletes feel less pain, giving them more **endurance**. The International Olympic Committee (IOC) takes the use of performance enhancing drugs very seriously. Regular testing of athletes helps ensure competitors do not use drugs to unnaturally improve their skills. Cross-country skiing requires a mixture of strength, speed, and endurance. Many performance enhancing drugs will help an athlete in one of these areas, but hurt them in others. For example, a drug may cause the heart to pump more blood to muscles in the arms, making the athlete physically stronger. This takes blood away from the heart and lungs, giving the athlete less endurance and slower long-term recovery. There are serious mental and physical health problems that arise from

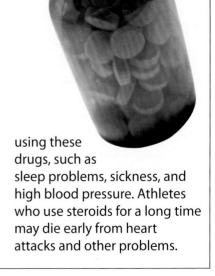

using these drugs, such as sleep problems, sickness, and high blood pressure. Athletes who use steroids for a long time may die early from heart attacks and other problems.

Exploring the Venue

The Whistler Olympic Park in British Columbia is the cross-country skiing venue for the 2010 Winter Olympic Games.

Olympic events are held in huge, specially built venues around the host city. These buildings can be used to exhibit one or multiple events and can cost more than $1 billion to build.

Cross-country skiing events at the Winter Olympics in 2010 will be held at Whistler Olympic Park in Whistler, British Columbia. This state-of-the-art facility was built especially to host the Winter Olympic Games. Aside from the Olympic cross-country skiing events, the park will host the biathlon, Nordic combined, and ski jumping competitions.

CEREMONIES

Two of the most-anticipated and popular events of the Olympics are the opening and closing ceremonies. These events are traditionally held in the largest venue that an Olympic host city can offer. Facilities such as football, baseball, or soccer stadiums are often used for these events. At the 2008 Olympic Games in Beijing, more than 90,000 people attended the opening ceremonies. The ceremonies are spectacular displays that include music, dancing, acrobatic stunts, and fireworks. The theme of the ceremonies usually celebrates the history and culture of the host nation and city. All of the athletes participating in the Olympics march into the stadium during the ceremonies. The athletes wave their country's flag and celebrate the achievement of competing in the Olympics.

vancouver 2010
February 12 to 28, 2010 · 12 au 28 février 2010

CROSS-COUNTRY SKIING
SKI DE FOND

vancouver 2010

The design on the tickets for the 2010 Olympic Winter Games reflects the natural landscape of Vancouver.

The venue cost $119.7 million to build, and will be used as a recreational and training facility before and after the Olympics in 2010.

Whistler Olympic Park has 10 kilometres of competition trails that consist of flat areas, rolling terrain, and hills. They will be used for all Olympic and Paralympic cross-country skiing events. As well, there are 35 kilometres of recreational and training trails. In the 50-kilometre event, competitors will climb a total of more than 610 metres uphill.

The start and finish lines of the trails are held at a 150-metre stadium that can hold 12,000 spectators per day. As well, Whistler Olympic Park includes a day lodge and a 6,000-square-foot technical building that is used for training, equipment maintenance and storage, and many other functions.

The day lodge at Whistler Olympic/Paralympic Park is located at the start area of the cross-country skiing stadium.

❧ **CANADIAN TIDBIT** The Olympic Stadium in Montreal is one of the most expensive stadiums ever built. By the time it was completely paid in 2006, the building had cost more than $1.4 billion.

Illustrating Cross-Country Skiing

SKATING STRIDE

The skier propels himself with both legs in a skating style. Sliding one leg forward, he pushes off on the other leg, which is placed at an angle to obtain a better push-off. He pushes sideways, off the inside edge of the ski. The slower the skier is going, the more propulsion is gained from the upper body.

DOUBLE POLING

Used for slight hills and on the flat. Both legs slide forward together, as the arms propel the skier. The movement begins with the body extending up and forward before the poles are planted. The push on the poles is started by bending the body and then the arms, forearms, and wrists. The skier lets himself fall forward. The body remains bent until the push with the poles is completed; then the arms are quickly brought forward.

DIAGONAL STRIDES

The skis must always be parallel and stay in the tracks, except in turns. Herringbone strides are used for climbing when the incline is steep.

1. PUSHING PHASE

The movement starts with a quick extension of the leg to push off, followed by the hip. The body leans forward and the ankle of the supporting leg is bent. The opposite arm and leg are then fully extended.

2. GLIDING PHASE

The shoulder and arm are stretched forward to plant the pole on the opposite side from the propelling leg. The body forms a straight line at the end of the push and the weight is transferred to the supporting ski as the other foot moves forward.

3. END OF MOVEMENT

The arms and poles return to the starting position.

SKIS

Light and solid, they are often made of woven carbon fibers with a honeycomb structure. Although skis are no longer made entirely of wood, it is always used to some extent because of its mechanical qualities. Skis are always taller than the skier; the heavier the skier, the stronger the instep must be.

FREESTYLE

They sometimes have a wider shovel to facilitate the skating movement, and the tips are less curved upward than are those for classical style. The harder the snow, the shorter the skis used.

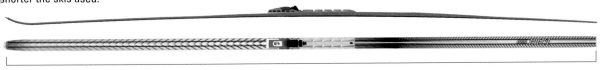

1.75 - 2 m

CLASSICAL STYLE

It is very important that the skis be rigid. They are longer than those used in freestyle to distribute the skier's weight more evenly.

RUNNING SURFACE

Identical in freestyle and classical skis, it is made of plastic and graphite with anti-static qualities for better gliding.

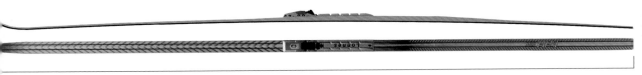

up to 2.20 m

Olympic Legends

OLYMPIC MEDALS WON

1 Gold   2 Silver   1 Bronze

Beckie Scott

Beckie Scott has appeared in three Olympic Winter Games. She retired after the 2006 Games in Turin, Italy.

Scott finished third in the 5-kilometre pursuit event in 2002. Later, her bronze medal was upgraded to silver and then gold after the first and second place winners were disqualified for using performance enhancing drugs.

Before she received the medals, Scott had to campaign to have the results of the pursuit overturned. The following year, the second place finisher was disqualified, and Scott was awarded the silver medal.

Scott continued to seek justice, and many FIS rules regarding performance enhancing drugs were changed as a result. More than two years after the Olympics, Scott was awarded the gold medal, Canada's first in cross-country skiing.

Scott also won the silver medal in the team relay in 2006. Today, she helps with planning and preparations for the 2010 Olympic Games in Vancouver. She works with children's charities, helping kids around the world participate in sports.

OLYMPIC MEDALS WON

2 Gold   3 Silver   5 Bronze

Stefania Belmondo

The greatest Italian cross-country skier is Stefania Belmondo. She has won a medal of every colour, including gold in the 30-kilometre event at the 1992 Winter Olympics in Albertville, France.

Competing in five total events in 1992, Belmondo finished in first, second, third, fourth, and fifth place, winning gold, silver, and bronze. She accomplished this in the presence of half of her hometown, who had travelled from Italy to watch her compete. Two years later, she won two more bronze medals at the Winter Olympics in Lillehammer, Norway. In Nagano, Japan, in 1998, Belmondo won a silver and a bronze medal.

In 2002, during her final Olympics appearance, Belmondo capped off her Olympic career by again winning medals of each colour. She took home bronze in the 10-kilometre, silver in the 30-kilometre, and gold in the 15-kilometre. In total, Belmondo competed in five Winter Olympics, winning 10 medals, including two gold, three silver, and five bronze medals.

Bjorn Daehlie

Bjorn Daehlie of Norway is the most successful Winter Olympic athlete in history. Daehlie competed in the Winter Olympics in 1992, 1994, and 1998. In those three appearances, Daehlie competed in 15 total events and won a total of 12 medals, the most medals won by any athlete in Winter Olympics history.

The first medal of Daehlie's Olympic career came in 1992, when he won the silver in the 3-kilometre event in Albertville, France. At the same Olympics, he won gold medals in the pursuit, 50-kilometre, and team relay events. In 1994, at the Winter Olympics in Lillehammer, Norway, Daehlie won silver in the 30-kilometre, his first gold in the 10-kilometre event, and a silver in relay. In 1998, in Nagano, Japan, Daehlie finished his Olympic career by winning the 10-kilometre event and placed second in the pursuit. The Norwegian team reclaimed the gold medal in the relay, and Daehlie finally won gold in the 50-kilometre event.

Bjorn Daehlie accomplished many feats that no one else has achieved. These include winning eight gold medals, six individual gold medals, and nine total individual medals.

FAST FACT

Bjorn Daehlie is the only athlete in the Winter Olympics to win eight gold medals.

OLYMPIC MEDALS WON

8 Gold   4 Silver

Thorleif Haug

At the first Winter Olympic Games, in 1924, Norwegian cross-country skier Thorleif Haug became a part of Olympic history. The 29-year old became the first cross-country skiing Olympic gold medalist. He won three gold medals in total, finishing in first place in both the 18-kilometre and 50-kilometre events, as well as the Nordic combined event.

Haug was the first Winter Olympian to win three gold medals in the same year.

At the 1924 Winter Olympics, Haug was awarded the bronze medal for finishing third in the ski jump competition. Fifty years later, a scoring error was discovered, and it was determined that Haug had actually finished in fourth place. Anders Haugen of the United States was the true bronze medalist. Since Haug had died in 1934, his daughter presented the bronze medal to then 86-year old Haugen.

FAST FACT

At the 1924 Games, Thorleif Haug was nicknamed the "King of Skis."

OLYMPIC MEDALS WON

3 Gold

WANT MORE?

For information about Canada's cross-country ski team, visit **www.cccski.com**.

Details about cross-country ski trails and equipment can be found at **www.xcski.org**.

Olympic Stars

PARALYMPIC MEDALS WON

4 Gold   2 Silver   1 Bronze

Brian McKeever

Brian McKeever, of Canmore, Alberta, hopes to become the first winter athlete to compete in both the Paralympics and Olympics. As a promising, young cross-country skier, McKeever competed in the 1998 World Junior Championship, the same year that his older brother Robin competed in the Winter Olympics. Later that year, Brian was diagnosed with Stargardt's disease, a condition that causes eyesight to slowly fade. He has continued skiing and has dominated **visually impaired** cross-country skiing events.

With Robin leading the way for the beginning part of races, Brian takes over for the final part of the races, sprinting to the finish line. Robin creates lines in the snow that Brian can follow, and he relays information about the trail to Brian as they ski. Using this strategy, Brian has won four gold medals, two silver, and one bronze at the Paralympic Games. In 2010, Brian and Robin will compete in the Paralympics. Brian also plans to compete in the Olympics. He competed in his first **able-bodied** event in 2007, finishing in 24th place. He was the top Canadian in the race.

OLYMPIC MEDALS WON

1 Silver

Sara Renner

In 2006, at the Winter Olympics in Turin, Italy, Sara Renner won a silver medal in the team sprint, alongside her teammate, Beckie Scott. Renner has been a member of the Canadian senior national cross-country skiing team for 13 years.

Renner began skiing at the age of four in Golden, British Columbia, and entered her first competition 10 years later. After only two years on the national junior team, Renner jumped to the senior team and has been competing for Canada on the world stage ever since.

Renner became the first Canadian to win a World Championship medal in cross-country skiing in 2005, when she won a bronze medal at a competition in Germany. The following year, she had her most successful season, winning four World Cup medals and the Olympic silver medal.

Training in Canmore, Alberta, along with her husband, former Canadian Olympic alpine skier, Thomas Grandi, Renner also works with the David Suzuki Foundation to help athletes reduce their **carbon emissions**.

Chandra Crawford

At the Winter Olympics in 2006, Chandra Crawford narrowly made the Canadian Olympic team. In 2005, she lost her place on the Canadian national 'A' team, which is the top team for Canadian skiers. Crawford worked hard to regain her place on the top team and earned a spot in the Olympics.

At a World Cup race in Sovereign Lakes, British Columbia, Crawford finished in 10th place in the sprint event. This result qualified her for the Olympics the following year.

Crawford continued to train, and two weeks before the 2006 Olympics, she won a bronze medal in the sprint event at a World Cup competition in Switzerland. Crawford then won the gold medal in the sprint event at the Olympics in 2006, becoming the second North American to win an Olympic gold medal in cross-country skiing. In 2008, she won her first World Cup in her hometown of Canmore, Alberta. When she is not training or competing, Chandra Crawford runs a program called Fast and Female, which helps young girls and women get involved in cross-country skiing.

FAST FACT

In the 2006–2007 season, Chandra Crawford won the gold medal in the Canadian Championships at Mont-Sainte-Anne in Quebec.

OLYMPIC MEDALS WON

1 Gold

Devon Kershaw

In 2006, Devon Kershaw competed in his first Winter Olympics, in Turin, Italy. Kershaw reached a milestone that year, becoming the first male Canadian cross-country skier to win a World Cup medal in more than 15 years. He won a bronze in the sprint event.

Kershaw has consistently finished near the top of sprint events at competitions as he prepares for the Winter Olympics in 2010. Training alongside his girlfriend, Chandra Crawford, Kershaw has been a competitive cross-country skier for 13 years. While skiing is his passion, Kershaw hopes to someday become a doctor.

FAST FACT

Devon Kershaw is considered to be one of the strongest sprint skiers in the world.

News about the 2010 Winter Olympics can be found by visiting **www.ctvolympics.ca/cross-country-skiing/index.html**.

For details about competitive and recreational skiing, go to **www.xcskiworld.com**.

A Day in the Life of an Olympic Athlete

Becoming an Olympic athlete takes a great deal of dedication and **perseverance**. Athletes must concentrate on remaining healthy and maximizing their strength and energy. Eating special foods according to a strict schedule, taking vitamins, waking up early to train and practise, and going to bed at a reasonable hour are important parts of staying in shape for world-class athletes. All athletes have different routines and training regimens. These regimens are suited to that athlete's body and lifestyle.

Eggs are a great source of **protein** and **iron**, and are low in **calories**, making them a popular breakfast choice. A cup of orange juice is a healthy breakfast drink, while coffee can give an athlete some extra energy in the morning. A light lunch, including a sandwich, yogurt, fruit, and juice, is usually a good option. This gives the body the right amount of energy, while it is not too filling. Chicken and pasta are popular dinnertime meals.

To enhance their performance, all athletes need to engage in rigorous training regimens.

Early Mornings

6:30 a.m.

Olympic athletes might wake up at 6:30 a.m. to record their resting **heart rate**. Next, they might stretch or perform yoga while their breakfast is being prepared. The first exercise of the day can happen before 7:00 a.m. Depending on an athlete's sport, the exercise routine can vary. Skiers might be in the gym lifting weights with their legs. After lifting weights for an hour, the athletes may move on to **aerobics** to help with strength and endurance.

Morning Practice

9:30 a.m.

By about 9:30 a.m., athletes are ready to practise their events. For a cross-country skier, this means putting on the skis and hitting the trails. Most Olympic athletes have coaches and trainers who help them develop training routines. After practice, skiers stretch to keep their muscles loose and avoid injuries. Many athletes use a sauna or an ice bath to help their muscles recover quickly.

Afternoon Nap

12:00 p.m.

At about noon, many athletes choose to take a break. Sleep helps the body and mind recover from stress. After waking up at 2:00 p.m., it is time for lunch and then, more exercise. **Core** exercises help skaters with stability. Speed exercises are also important for skiers. A cross-country skier's legs must be especially strong. Working out leg muscles is an important part of training for skiers.

Dinnertime

6:00 p.m.

After the afternoon workout, it is dinnertime. Another healthy meal helps athletes recover from the day and prepares their bodies for the next day's training. The evening can be spent relaxing and doing more light stretches. It is important for athletes to rest after a hard day of training so that they can do their challenging routine again the next day.

Olympic Volunteers

The call for 25,000 volunteers for the 2010 Olympics in Vancouver was launched on February 12, 2008.

Volunteers help in everything from shovelling snow to doing other tasks that will help the Olympians to perform at their best.

Volunteers are an important part of creating an enjoyable Olympic experience for athletes and spectators. Thousands of volunteers help organize and execute the Olympic Games. Olympic volunteers are enthusiastic, committed, and dedicated to helping welcome the world to the host city. Volunteers help prepare for the Olympics in the years leading up to the events and even after the Olympics are over.

Before the Olympics begin, many countries send representatives to the host city to view event venues and plans. Olympic volunteers help make the representatives' stay enjoyable. From meeting these representatives at the airport, showing them around the city and the surrounding areas, and providing accommodations and **transportation**, volunteers make life easier for visitors to the host city.

🍁 **CANADIAN TIDBIT** The Olympics in Vancouver will be relying on about 25,000 volunteers to make the Games a memorable, enjoyable experience for athletes, judges, spectators, and officials from all over the world.

During the Olympics, volunteers help in many different areas. During the opening, closing, and medal ceremonies, volunteers help prepare costumes, props, and performers for the events. Editorial volunteers help by preparing written materials for use in promoting events and on the official website of the Olympics. Food and beverage volunteers provide catering services to athletes, judges, officials, spectators, and media.

Some volunteers get a chance to view events and work with competitors. Anti-doping volunteers notify athletes when they have been selected for drug testing. These volunteers explain the process to the athletes and escort them to the drug-testing facility. Other volunteers become involved with the sporting events by helping to maintain the venues and the fields of play, providing medical assistance to athletes, transporting athletes to events, and helping with the set-up and effective running of events.

Torch Relay

One of the most anticipated events of each Olympics is the torch relay. The torch is lit during a ritual in Olympia, Greece, before it is flown to the host nation. The torch is then carried along a route across the country until it reaches the host city during the opening ceremonies. The torch relay for 2010 covers 45,000 kilometres over 106 days. The relay will begin in Victoria before moving through communities in all 10 Canadian provinces and three territories. About 12,000 volunteers will be chosen to carry the torch across Canada. Other volunteers help drive and maintain the vehicles that accompany the torch on its journey.

The torch relay represents the courage, determination, and the extraordinary achievements of the Olympians.

What are the Paralympics?

First held in 1960, the Paralympic Games are a sports competition for disabled competitors. Like the Olympics, the Paralympics celebrate the athletic achievements of its competitors. The Paralympics are held in the same year and city as the Olympics. Many sports appear in both the Paralympics and the Olympics, such as swimming, nordic skiing, and alpine skiing. The Paralympics also feature wheelchair basketball, **goalball**, and ice sledge hockey. The first Winter Paralympic Games were held in 1976.

Athletes competing at the Paralympics are classified by disability in six categories, including **amputee**, **cerebral palsy**, visual impairment, **spinal cord** injuries, **intellectual disability**, and a group for other disabilities. These classifications allow athletes to compete in a fair and equal basis in each event. Goalball, for example, is a sport for the visually impaired, and not for amputees.

Mono skiers need to use the greatest amount of coordination, balance, and strength in their performance.

Paralympians use special equipment that will help to protect their bodies as well as enhance the quality of their performance.

There is no limit to what Paralympians can achieve in the sports arena.

Nordic skiing, which includes biathlon and cross-country skiing, can be done by athletes with physical disabilities or visual impairment. Skiers with lower body disabilities use a device called a sit-ski, which is a chair that attaches to a pair of skis. Visually impaired competitors are guided through the course by a partner who is not visually impaired.

In biathlon, visually impaired competitors use a special rifle that allows them to aim by sound, rather than by sight. As the skier moves closer to the target, the sound coming from the rifle gets higher. Canadian cross-country skier, Brian McKeever, along with his guide and brother, Robin, have competed in two Paralympic Winter Games. Robin competed for Canada in the Olympics in 1998 and is a nine-time Canadian champion.

The parade of athletes at the opening ceremony is one of the proudest moments for all athletes participating in the Olympics/Paralympics.

Olympics and the Environment

Hosting so many people in one city can be costly to the environment. Host cities often build new venues and roads to accommodate the Games. For example, a great deal of transportation is needed to support construction projects, planning for the games, and to move the athletes, participants, volunteers, media, and spectators around the host city and its surrounding areas. This transportation causes pollution.

In recent years, the IOC and Olympic host cities have been working to make the Olympics more green. With their beautiful surroundings, including the Pacific Ocean to the West and the Rocky Mountains to the East, Vancouver and Whistler have taken many steps to protect the environment.

As host city of the 2010 Winter Olympics, Vancouver is taking measures to reduce harmful effects to the environment.

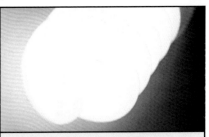

WHISTLER SLIDING CENTRE

At the Whistler Sliding Centre, home to the bobsleigh, luge, and skeleton events, an ice plant is used to keep the ice frozen. The heat waste from this plant is used to heat other buildings in the area. All wood waste from the Whistler sites will be chipped, composted, and reused on the same site.

LIL'WAT ABORIGINAL NATION

Working with the Lil'wat Aboriginal Nation, builders of the Olympic cross-country ski trails created venues that could be used long after the Olympics. About 50 kilometres of trails have been built that can be used by cross-country skiers and hikers of all skill levels.

VANCOUVER LIGHTING AND HEATING SYSTEMS

Venues in Whistler and Vancouver have been equipped with efficient lighting and heating systems. These systems reduce the amount of **greenhouse gases** released into the atmosphere during the Olympics.

GREENHOUSE GASES

Half of the organizing committee's vehicles are either **hybrid** or equipped with fuel management technology. These vehicles emit less greenhouse gases than other vehicles. As well, venues have been made accessible to users of transit, and many event tickets include transit tickets to promote mass transportation at the games.

VANCOUVER CONVENTION AND EXHIBITION CENTRE

The Vancouver Convention and Exhibition Centre uses a seawater heating system. This system uses the surrounding natural resources to make the building a more comfortable place to visit. The centre also houses a fish habitat.

RICHMOND OLYMPIC OVAL

The Richmond Olympic Oval was built with a wooden arced ceiling. The huge amount of wood needed to build the ceiling was reclaimed from forests that have been destroyed by mountain pine beetles. These beetles feed on pine trees, killing them in the process. Using this wood helps stop other, healthy trees from being cut down for construction materials.

🍁 **CANADIAN TIDBIT** The 2010 Games are estimated to cost more than $4 billion, including about $2.5 billion of taxpayer money.

Steady Ski Poles

Cross-country skiers use poles to help push themselves along and stabilize their bodies. In the past, skiers used one long pole, which they would dig into the snow on either side of their body. Today, skiers use two smaller poles. What do you think are the advantages of using two poles instead of one?

What you need

ice skates or rollerblades
a pair of hockey sticks, brooms,
    or long branches
a sheet of ice or a smooth surface

1. First, put on the ice skates or rollerblades, and use one pole to push yourself along the ice or smooth surface. Do not push with your legs. Is this difficult or easy? How does your body feel when you do this?

2. Now, do the same using the two hockey sticks, brooms, or branches to push yourself forward. Is this easier or more difficult? Does it feel like you are using different muscles?

3. Next, try taking a few strides while pushing yourself along with the single pole. With each stride, push the pole into the ground on the opposite side of your body. Do you notice any differences? Does any one technique help you move faster? Is any technique easier on your muscles? Think about how this would help when racing or travelling a long distance.

Further Research

Visit Your Library

Many books and websites provide information on cross-country skiing. To learn more about cross-country skiing, borrow books from the library, or surf the Internet.

Most libraries have computers that connect to a database when researching information. If you input a topic, you will be provided with a list of books in the library that contain information on that topic. Nonfiction books are arranged numerically, using their call number. Fiction books are organized alphabetically by the author's last name.

Surf the Web

Learn more about cross-country skiing by visiting **www.olympic.org/uk/sports/programme/disciplines _uk.asp?DiscCode=CC.**

To learn all about Paralympic Nordic skiing, visit **www.paralympic.org/release/Winter_Sports/Nordic_Skiing /About_the_sport.**

Glossary

able-bodied: an athlete who does not have a disability

aerobics: exercise for the heart and lungs

aerodynamic: reducing the amount of drag from air resistance

amateur: an athlete who does not receive money for competing

amputee: a person who has had a body part of his or her body removed

biathlon: a sport in which athletes combine cross-country skiing and target shooting skills

calories: units of energy, especially in food

carbon emissions: greenhouse gases released into the atmosphere

cerebral palsy: a condition that typically causes impaired muscle coordination

core: the trunk of the body, including the hips and torso

disciplines: subdivisions within a sport that require different skills, training, or equipment

endurance: the ability to continue doing something that is difficult

goalball: a sport for blind athletes; the ball used makes noise, helping blind athletes locate it

greenhouse gases: gases that are trapped within Earth's atmosphere by the greenhouse effect

heart rate: the number of times the heart beats in one minute

hybrid: a vehicle that uses a combination of fuels

intellectual disability: a disability that hampers the function of the mind

iron: a substance in foods that is good for the blood

nordic combined: an event that combines the skills of cross-country skiing and ski jumping

perseverance: a commitment to doing a task despite challenges that arise in the process

protein: a substance needed by the body to build healthy muscles

pursuit: an event that requires a change of skis and styles mid-race

Scandinavia: the area of northern Europe containing the countries of Denmark, Norway, and Sweden

spinal cord: a bundle of nerves held inside the spine, connecting almost all parts of the body to the brain

transportation: the use of vehicles to move people

visually impaired: not being able to see well

Index